When Posey Peeked at Christmas

Dec. 24

Ann Dixon

Illustrated by Anne Kennedy

Albert Whitman & Company, Morton Grove, Illinois

For Walter, who never peeks.–A.D.

To Dawn, my Christmas sister.–A.K.

Library of Congress Cataloging-in-Publication Data

Dixon, Ann.
When Posey peeked at Christmas / by Ann Dixon ; illustrated by Anne Kennedy.
p. cm.
Summary: At Christmas time, Grandma Mouse shares a story of a little girl who peeks at her gifts the night
before Christmas Eve, then feels terrible about what she has done.
ISBN 978-0-8075-8919-9
[1. Behavior–Fiction. 2. Gifts–Fiction. 3. Christmas–Fiction. 4. Mice–Fiction. 5. Grandmothers–Fiction.]
I. Kennedy, Anne, 1955- ill. II. Title.
PZ7.D642Whe 2008 [E]–dc22 2008000281

The illustrations were done in watercolors, ink, and dyes.
The design is by Carol Gildar.

For more information about Albert Whitman & Company, visit our web site at www.albertwhitman.com.

It was Christmas in the mousehole.

The sweet aroma of honey and wild ginger drifted out from
the kitchen, where Mama Mouse was busy baking. Papa Mouse
carried in firewood and kissed Mama under the mistletoe.

In the sitting room, Grandma and the youngsters were decorating a handsome, piney tree.

"Grandma, what's that?" asked little Forrest.

"It's my favorite ornament," said Grandma. She held up a small box, wrapped with faded paper and ribbon.

"Why is it your favorite?" asked Holly, the middle mouse. "You can't even read what's written on it anymore."

"What's inside?" asked Malva, the oldest.

A smile, like a lovely secret, twitched across Grandma's
whiskers. "Why, a story, I'd say. A Christmas story."

The mice squeaked. "Tell it, Grandma. Please!"

"If you insist," agreed Grandma.

Once there was a young mouse named Posey, who absolutely loved Christmas. She loved the music, the decorations, the food, the lights. Most of all, she loved the presents.

Each year on Christmas Eve, the family opened their presents from Grandma, Grandpa, and dear Aunt Lily. Posey could hardly wait. She sniffed and shook and squeezed each present over and over.

"Posey, stop that snooping!" her mother would say.

But Posey would not stop.

One year, on the afternoon of Christmas Eve, Mama, Papa,
and little sister Tansy went caroling. Posey stayed behind with a cold.
The mousehole was very quiet. Posey looked at all the lovely
presents. She began sorting through them, pulling out her own.
Soon she was sniffing, shaking, and squeezing again.

As she poked at one package, the end of the wrapping paper popped loose. She lifted the flap, but couldn't see inside.
She loosened the other flap. Still, she couldn't see inside.

She slid the box out of the paper and opened it. Inside was a party dress in blue and yellow, Posey's favorite colors.

The dress was beautiful.

Then she loosened the wrapping on her other presents.

She found a pair of fuzzy yellow slippers; the next book in the Mousey Girl series; and a set of bright, shiny paints.

Posey was thrilled with each gift.

When she was done looking, she rewrapped the packages . . .

and placed them back under the tree.

When the family came home, Posey grew
uneasy. No one knew about the peeking, yet Posey
felt as if written on her forehead, in big red letters,
were the words: I PEEKED!

Still, Posey said nothing. Even when Mama
asked, "Has someone rearranged the presents?"

Even when Papa said, "Some of the
wrapping paper has come loose."

Even when Tansy asked, "Santa Mouse doesn't come if you peek, does he?"

Santa Mouse! How could she have forgotten? Surely now he would not bring her the doll she wanted. He might not bring her any presents at all. He might leave a lump of grimy coal in her stocking!

At Christmas Eve supper,
Posey barely touched her cheese pie.
She nibbled only the ears of her
gingerbread mouse.

"Are you feeling all right?"
asked Mama.

"I'm just not hungry," said Posey.
But Posey wasn't feeling at all right.

When it came time to light the candles and open presents, Tansy cheered, Papa joked, and Mama giggled. Posey tried to squeal with delight as she opened her presents, but she could only pretend to share in the fun. For Posey there were no surprises.

Even her new dress no longer looked so beautiful.

It was the worst Christmas Eve of Posey's life.

That night, Posey slept fitfully. What if Santa left her an ugly lump of coal?

Early Christmas morning, Tansy jumped out of bed. "Hurry up!" she squealed. "Let's see what Santa brought!"

Tansy raced downstairs. Posey lagged behind.

A fresh pile of presents waited under the tree. And there was something for Posey from Santa, after all!

Posey ripped off the paper. It was the doll she wanted!
The most beautiful doll in the world.

Tansy checked her stocking. "Look!" she cried. "New socks! Tail ribbons! Comic books! And licorice sticks— my favorite!"

Posey saw a bulge in her stocking, too. Was it black grimy coal?

Trembling, Posey peeked inside.

"Hooray!" she squeaked. "Santa brought me socks!
Tail ribbons! Comic books! Butterscotch sticks!
And—and—what's this?"

It was a small box. "DO NOT OPEN TILL CHRISTMAS" was written on the outside.

"Open it," said Tansy.

"No," said Posey.

"Why not?" asked Tansy. "It's Christmas."

"Because some things are better if you wait," said Posey.

And that's just what Posey did. She saved the red box
until next Christmas, and the next Christmas, and the next.
Year after year after year.

Grandma stopped. She'd finished her story.

The mice shrieked and wiggled their tails. "You mean she never, ever opened it?" asked Holly.

"What's inside?" demanded Forrest.

"But Grandma, *your* name is Posey!" said Malva.

A smile, like a happy ending, spread across Grandma's face. She hung the faded little box up high on the tree.

"Merry Christmas, children!" she exclaimed.

And she gathered them up in a great big holiday hug.